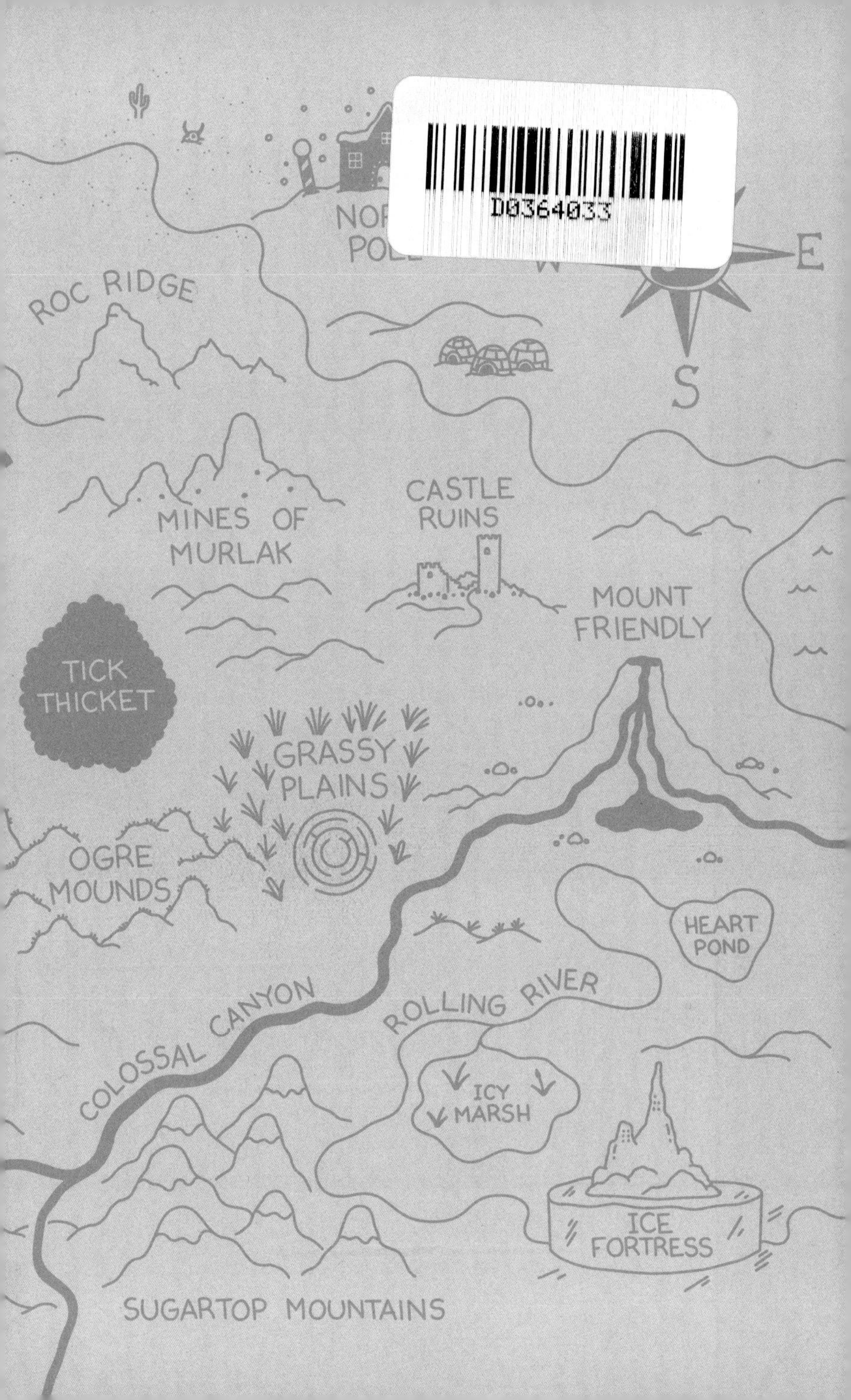
NOR
POL
E
S
ROC RIDGE
MINES OF
MURLAK
CASTLE
RUINS
MOUNT
FRIENDLY
TICK
THICKET
GRASSY
PLAINS
OGRE
MOUNDS
HEART
POND
ROLLING RIVER
COLOSSAL CANYON
ICY
MARSH
ICE
FORTRESS
SUGARTOP MOUNTAINS

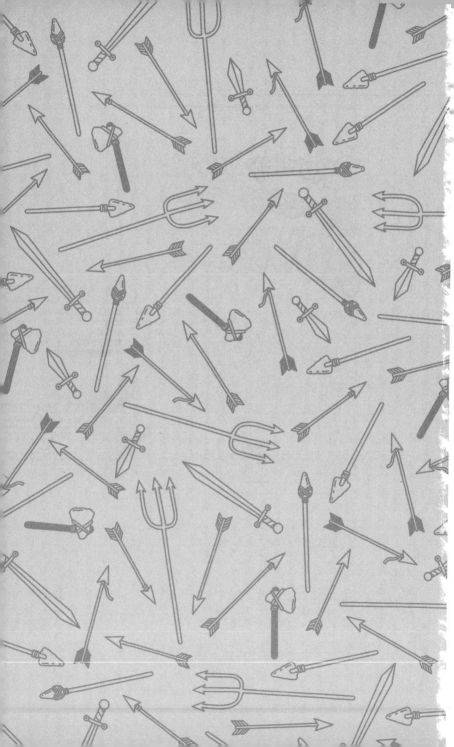

PUFFIN BOOKS

Rowley Jefferson's Awesome Friendly ADVENTURE

ALSO BY ROWLEY JEFFERSON

Diary of an Awesome Friendly Kid

GREG HEFFLEY'S
DIARY OF A WIMPY KID BOOKS

Rowley Jefferson's Awesome Friendly ADVENTURE

by Jeff Kinney

PUFFIN

PUFFIN BOOKS

UK | USA | Canada | Ireland | Australia
India | New Zealand | South Africa

Puffin Books is part of the Penguin Random House group of companies
whose addresses can be found at global.penguinrandomhouse.com.

www.penguin.co.uk   www.puffin.co.uk   www.ladybird.co.uk

First published in the USA in the English language in 2020
by Amulet Books, an imprint of ABRAMS
(All rights reserved in all countries by Harry N. Abrams, Inc.)
Published simultaneously in Great Britain by Puffin Books 2020

001

Cover design by Jeff Kinney and Marcie Lawrence
Book design by Jeff Kinney

Printed and bound in Great Britain by Clays Ltd, Elcograf S.p.A

A CIP catalogue record for this book is available from the British Library

ISBN: 978–0–241–45881–5

All correspondence to:
Puffin Books, Penguin Random House Children's
One Embassy Gardens, New Union Square
5 Nine Elms Lane, London SW8 5DA

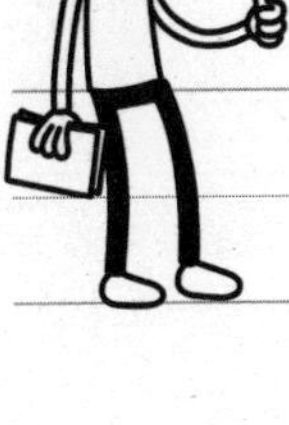

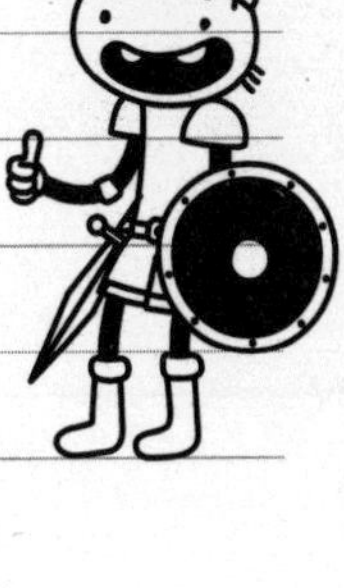

CHAPTER 1

Once upon a time in a land far away there lived a boy named Roland. And Roland was a very good boy.

Back then school hadn't been invented yet so most kids worked on their family farms all day.

But Roland's parents thought it was important for their son to get an education and to learn to play an instrument. So he spent his days inside, reading books and practising the flute.

Roland didn't like practising the flute very much but he never complained because he wanted to be a good son.

It was a dangerous time when ogres and giants roamed the land. So Roland's parents liked him to stay indoors where it was safe, especially after dark.

TIME TO COME INSIDE NOW ROLAND.

Roland had never even been outside his village. He wished he could go on adventures like his grandpa Bampy the Brave who used to fight monsters and search for treasure.

But Bampy was never the same after he got back from his adventures. And Roland knew that was because Bampy didn't always wear his helmet and he got hit on the head a few too many times.

Roland promised his parents that if he went on an adventure he'd ALWAYS wear a helmet and he'd make good choices. But they said he'd be much safer staying at home and practising his flute.

So the only thing Roland could do was read stories about Bampy and imagine what it would be like to have adventures of his OWN.

Sometimes after Roland read about the monsters in Bampy's stories he'd get kind of SCARED and then he'd have to sleep in his parents' bed for a few nights. But his parents probably didn't mind because they loved him very much.

Most of the time Roland's dad worked from home but once or twice a month he'd go on a business trip to another village. And Roland's dad would always say the same thing when he left.

Right about now you're probably thinking "So far this is a pretty boring book." But just wait because in a second it's about to get really GOOD.

This one morning when Roland's dad was on one of his trips something totally CRAZY happened. Roland woke up early to practise his flute but then it got really COLD in his room.

And when he looked out of the window he couldn't believe it was SNOWING.

Oh yeah I probably should've mentioned that this was the middle of summer because then you'd be even MORE amazed.

Roland ran down to the kitchen to tell his mom about the snow but he couldn't find her ANYWHERE.

So Roland went outside to ask his neighbour Mrs Nettles where his mom was because Mrs Nettles was pretty nosy and she always knew everybody's business.

But that's when Roland got some really bad news.

Mrs Nettles said the White Warlock
came to the village and KIDNAPPED
Roland's mom. And he took her to his Ice
Fortress where he was keeping her as his
PRISONER.

Now Roland was TOTALLY FREAKED OUT.
You're probably thinking "Well why didn't
Roland just call his dad?"

But guess what? Phones weren't invented
yet so he COULDN'T.

Plus if Roland mailed his dad a letter to
tell him what happened it wouldn't get
to him for a long time because back then
the mail took FOREVER.

Roland was worried about his mom but he
was ALSO worried what his dad was going
to say when he got home from his trip.

I AM VERY DISAPPOINTED IN YOU SON.

Roland decided the only thing he COULD
do was travel to the Ice Fortress and
rescue his mom on his OWN.

But Roland knew the journey was going to be dangerous so he went down to the basement and got Bampy's old armour out of a musty chest.

And even though Roland was a little nervous about monsters and sad about his mom getting kidnapped he was also EXCITED because he was about to go on his first ADVENTURE.

After I wrote the first chapter of my book I showed it to my mom who said she was proud of me for using my imagination. Then she said she couldn't wait to find out what happens NEXT.

I haven't shown it to my dad yet because I wanna FINISH it first. And when I'm done I'm gonna ask him to read it to me as my bedtime story. But I'll pretend I don't know what's gonna happen so it'll still be SPECIAL.

I was pretty excited to show the book
to my best friend Greg Heffley because
he likes stories with dragons and wizards
and that kind of stuff and I figured he'd
think it was pretty awesome.

But I couldn't really tell if he liked it or
not because at first he didn't say much.

I asked Greg what he thought of the
story so far and he asked me if I wanted
his honest opinion or if he should tell me
what I WANTED to hear. And I said I
wanted his honest opinion.

But Greg reminded me that the LAST time I asked for his honest opinion it got him in TROUBLE. That was the time I showed him my tap-dancing routine after taking my first lesson.

Greg told me he thought it was terrible and that hurt my feelings. So I told his mom what he said and she wasn't happy.

Greg said if he told me his honest opinion about my book and it hurt my feelings I wasn't allowed to go running to his mom. So I said OK and we did a pinky swear.

After that was settled Greg told me all the things that were wrong with my story. And boy he had a LOT to say.

The first thing he said is that I can't start the book with "Once upon a time" because that's corny and it makes it sound like a fairy tale. And that kind of hurt my feelings right away because it's SUPPOSED to be a fairy tale.

Then Greg said no offence but this Roland character has got a lot of problems and the biggest one is his HAIR.

He said Roland has a mullet which is the worst type of haircut a person can have. I said the reason Roland's hair is long in the back is so he'll look cool when he does action stuff.

And Greg said maybe Roland can get a haircut at the beginning of Chapter Two.

Then Greg said no offence but Roland kind of seems like a BABY and it's not really believable that a kid his age would sleep in his parents' bed.

And that made me feel a little ashamed because sometimes I sleep in my parents' bed, especially on nights when there's a really bad thunderstorm.

Greg taught me a long time ago that if you say "no offence" then the other person isn't allowed to have hurt feelings about what you say AFTER it.

But I think that only works with kids because one time I tried it on my dad and he got mad.

NO OFFENCE BUT YOUR BREATH STINKS.

Greg said the book was gonna be too boring if it was only about Roland and that he needed a SIDEKICK. I said maybe Roland could have a best friend who goes WITH him and his name could be Greg Heffley.

But he told me everything about his life is "copyright Greg Heffley" and if I used his name I'd have to pay him MONEY. So I decided to make up a different sidekick for Roland because I don't want any trouble with Greg.

Greg said he didn't know if he could read a book about a boy who has to rescue his mom because that's a little too WEIRD. So I said maybe I could switch Roland's mom for a PRINCESS and Roland could rescue her INSTEAD.

But Greg said nowadays princesses are tough and know how to fight so they don't NEED some guy to rescue them.

He said if I wrote a book about a helpless princess who needs to be saved by some dude then I'm gonna get a ton of angry letters.

Well that got me kind of worried because I don't WANNA get a bunch of angry letters. But Greg said I could put my publisher's address on the back of the book and then all the angry letters would go to THEM.

I said I was just writing the book for MYSELF and that I wasn't really TRYING to get it published. But Greg said if I was gonna do all this work I might as well try to cash in.

He said that if my book gets published
I'll have to think about movies and toys
and T-shirts and swimwear and all sorts
of OTHER stuff too. And that sounded
complicated.

Then Greg said he'd make me a DEAL. He
said I could focus on the writing and he'd
handle everything ELSE. Then we'd split
all the profits fifty-fifty.

I was excited because that meant me
and Greg were gonna be PARTNERS. So
we did another pinky swear to make it
OFFICIAL.

CHAPTER 2

Even though Roland felt pretty brave wearing Bampy's armour, he was still kind of scared to leave his village all by himself.

So Roland went to see if his friend Garg the Barbarian wanted to come WITH him.

Roland met Garg when they were both little kids and ever since then they have been

Since Garg was a barbarian he was always using his muscles to smash things. And that's why Roland's parents didn't let Garg come to their house for sleepovers.

Garg's parents didn't make him read
books or play the flute so mostly Garg
just worked out in his garage. And
sometimes Roland worked out WITH him.

Since Garg didn't read a lot of books he
didn't know that many words. But Roland
always understood him anyway.

Roland told Garg that the White Warlock kidnapped his mom and that he needed some help RESCUING her. And Garg didn't even ask his parents for permission to go because they never really cared what he did anyway.

But before Roland and Garg could leave for their trip they needed to go to the village shop and get some SUPPLIES.

Roland used his allowance to buy a bunch of food and torches and camping stuff. Then Garg picked out some things HE wanted to bring on the trip.

Roland asked Garg to chip in but as usual
Garg didn't have any money.

The guy at the shop said Garg was going
to need some armour if they were going on
a dangerous journey but Roland explained
that Garg doesn't wear a lot of clothes
because he likes to show off his muscles.

Roland used his last gold coins to pay for
a map of the world outside the village.
And even though Roland was nervous
about leaving the village that he'd lived in
his whole life he was pretty excited too.

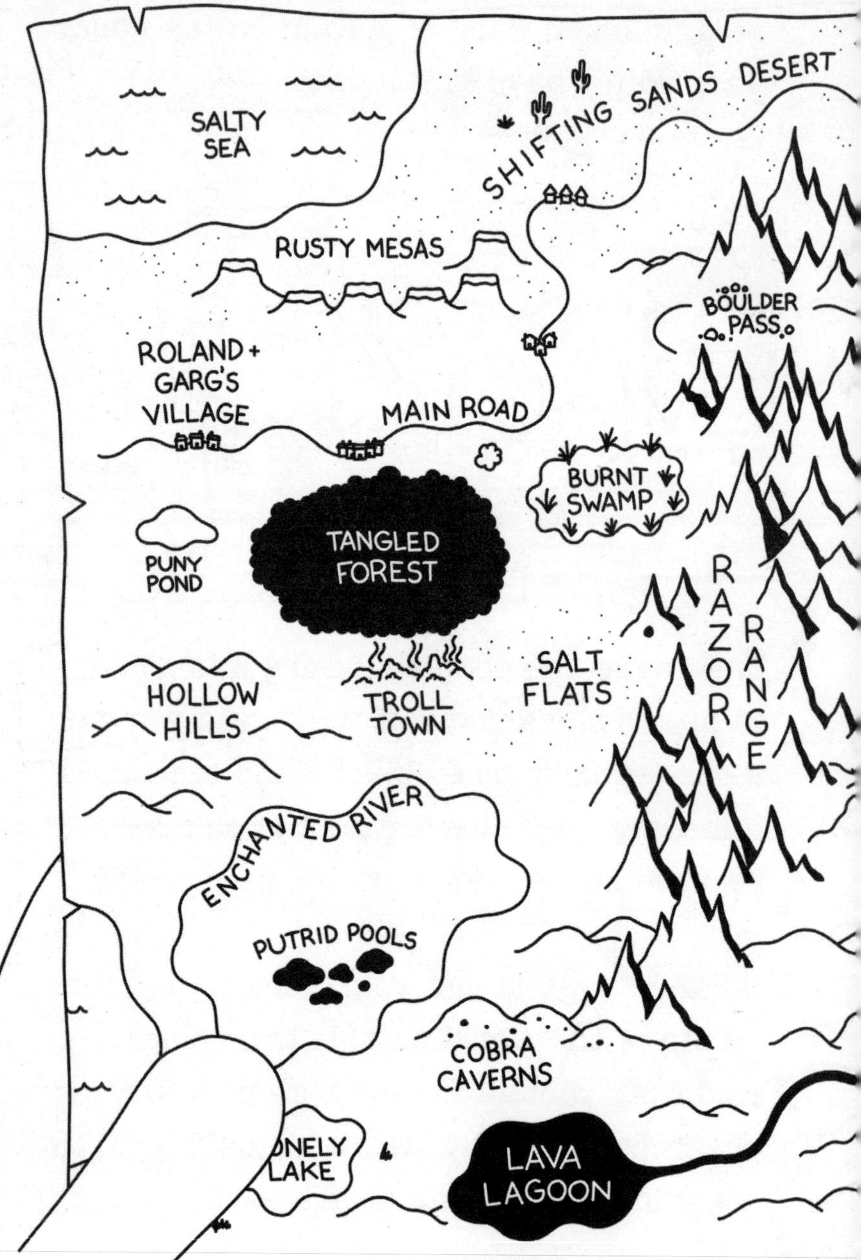
SALTY SEA
SHIFTING SANDS DESERT
RUSTY MESAS
BOULDER PASS
ROLAND + GARG'S VILLAGE
MAIN ROAD
BURNT SWAMP
TANGLED FOREST
PUNY POND
RAZOR RANGE
SALT FLATS
HOLLOW HILLS
TROLL TOWN
ENCHANTED RIVER
PUTRID POOLS
COBRA CAVERNS
LAVA LAGOON
LAKE

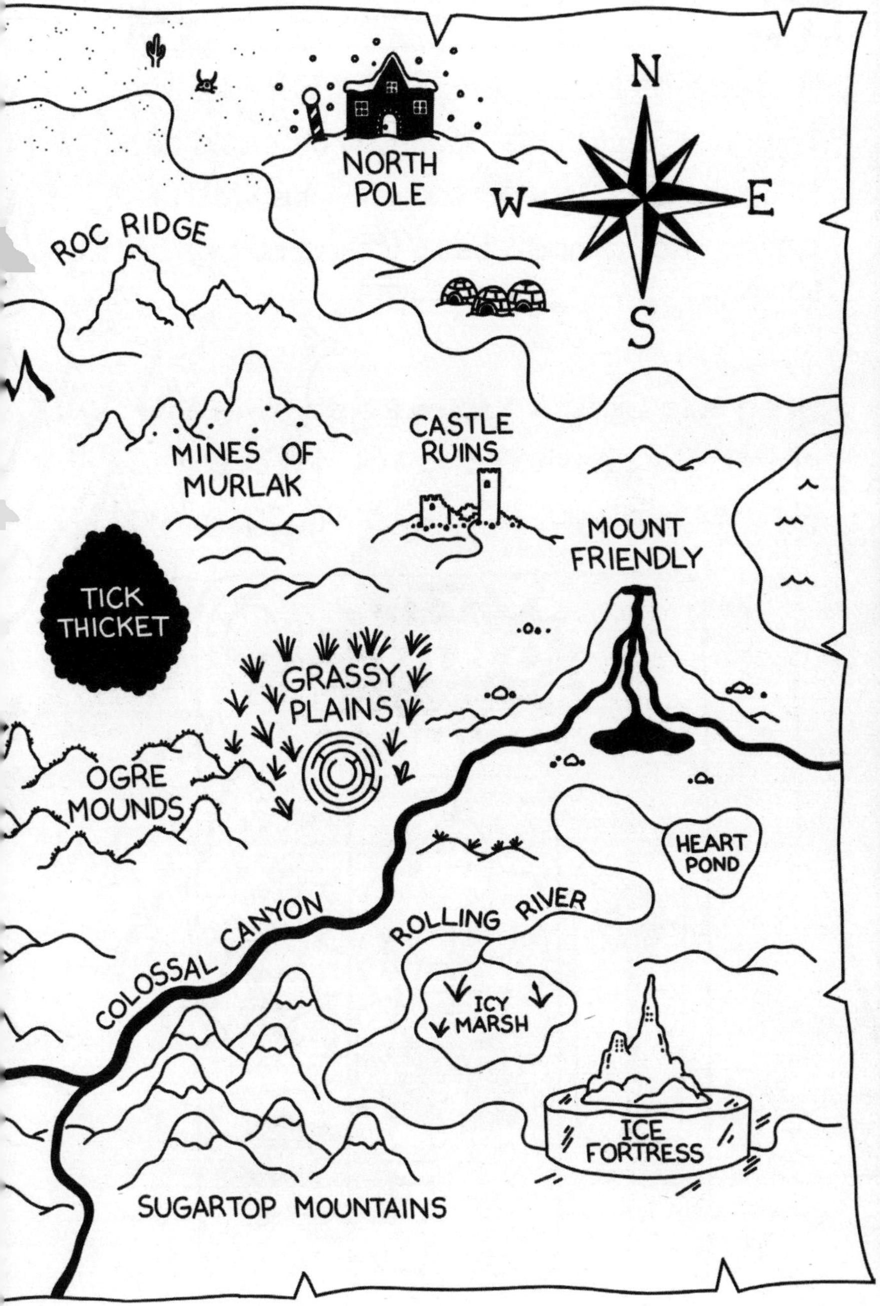
N
E
S
W
NORTH POLE
ROC RIDGE
MINES OF MURLAK
CASTLE RUINS
MOUNT FRIENDLY
TICK THICKET
GRASSY PLAINS
OGRE MOUNDS
HEART POND
COLOSSAL CANYON
ROLLING RIVER
ICY MARSH
ICE FORTRESS
SUGARTOP MOUNTAINS

As soon as I was done with Chapter Two I took it to Greg's house so he could read it. I was a little worried that he wasn't gonna like Roland's best friend but he thought Garg was GREAT.

Greg said Garg would make an awesome action figure who could say different phrases when you pressed down on his head.

I said maybe Roland could be an action figure TOO but Greg said no one would buy a Roland toy because he's just a regular kid and he doesn't really do a lot.

PEASANT

ACTION FIGURE

WITH FLUTE

Then I said maybe Roland could be a young WIZARD who has a wand and casts spells. But Greg said I needed to come up with something BETTER because no one would read a book about a boy wizard.

Greg said Roland needed to be TOUGH like Garg. He said boys would like Garg but girls would be in LOVE with him and they'd put Garg posters in their bedrooms.

Then Greg said when they make the MOVIE they'll have to bring in bodybuilders to try out for the part of Garg.

I said maybe girls would put posters of ROLAND up in their bedrooms too. And Greg said yeah maybe after Roland hits puberty and gets braces.

Greg told me once I finish this book I should write a PREQUEL where Garg is a BABY. And that way we could sell dolls and make millions of dollars.

But what Greg was MOST excited about was the MAP. He said it was great that there were a ton of different environments because that meant we could get kids to buy the same action figures a bunch of times.

And Greg said we could sell all sorts of playsets for the action figures because that's where the REAL money is.

He said his only problem with the map is that it doesn't make a whole lot of SENSE. He said I can't have a desert right next to a place that's snowy because that's not the way things work in real life.

Plus he said there were some things I was gonna have to fix like the river that went in a CIRCLE since that's not even physically possible.

But I said it was a LAZY river and it's MAGIC. And I told him my story is FANTASY so it doesn't HAVE to make sense anyway.

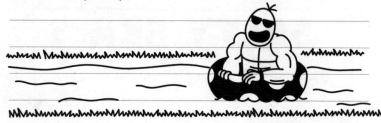

Greg said if this is supposed to be fantasy then I can't have REAL places on the map like the North Pole.

But I told him I put the North Pole on there because I'm hoping Roland and Garg might get to visit Santa Claus at his workshop.

Greg said if I put Santa Claus in the story he was gonna QUIT.

Then Greg told me he didn't really CARE what was on the map as long as the next chapter's not just about Garg and Roland SHOPPING. And I told Greg not to worry because now the adventure is about to start for REAL.

But hopefully Roland and Garg get to meet Santa somewhere on their journey because that would be pretty cool.

CHAPTER 3

Roland and Garg left their village behind and started out on their adventure.

On the first day they walked for miles and miles. Garg's feet were as tough as leather so all that walking didn't bother him.

But Roland's feet were soft and tender from spending most of his time indoors and he got a blister on his heel after a few hours and needed Garg to carry him.

That night Garg and Roland pitched their tents and sat by the campfire.

Whenever Roland got a blister or a splinter back home his mom always made him feel better. And thinking about his mom made Roland very sad.

The next morning Roland and Garg came to a village that was just like theirs.

But the road was blocked by boulders because there was an avalanche the night before. Roland offered to help clear the road and the villagers said "Sure."

So Garg and Roland spent the rest of the day moving heavy rocks which wasn't as easy as Roland thought it would be.

That night the villagers gave Roland and Garg a hot meal and soft beds to sleep in. And in the morning Roland and Garg packed up their things so they could get back on the road.

But the villagers told Roland and Garg there was something ELSE they needed help with before they headed out.

The villagers said the stables were a total mess because nobody had cleaned them in YEARS.

So they asked Roland and Garg if they could tidy the place up a little bit. And that was hard work too.

It took a lot longer than Roland expected and by the time they were done it was night-time again. And Roland and Garg slept very well that night because all the cleaning had totally wiped them out.

But by the morning the villagers had a whole LIST of things for them to do. And since Roland liked to be helpful him and Garg stuck around for another day.

Sometimes the villagers asked Roland and Garg to do stuff that Roland thought the villagers should've been able to do THEMSELVES.

But whenever Roland mentioned that to the villagers they always said the same thing.

And even after Roland TAUGHT them how to do something they STILL didn't get it. But if you're thinking "Gosh those villagers were pretty dumb" well remember this is back before schools were invented so there were a LOT of things people didn't know.

Even though Roland really wanted to get going he stayed and kept helping out in the village because he knew that would make his mom proud.

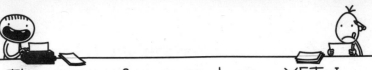

This was my favourite chapter YET. I
told Greg that parents would probably
like reading this story to their KIDS
because Roland was such a good role
model for young people.

But Greg said kids would think Roland
was a SUCKER for doing all the villagers'
work FOR them.

I said Roland isn't a sucker he just likes
being HELPFUL. And Greg said if Roland
helps every person he meets on his
journey then this book is gonna be like a
thousand pages long.

I told Greg that Roland ALWAYS helps
people in need because that's how his
parents RAISED him.

And Greg said well if Superman helped
everyone who ASKED he'd never be able
to RELAX.

Greg said maybe Roland and Garg should get off the main road for a while so they don't run into any more villagers who needed their help.

He said this book is supposed to be an ADVENTURE but right now it's just two guys doing a bunch of CHORES.

Then Greg said if this story's gonna be any GOOD I was gonna have to put some MONSTERS in it.

SHUDDER
SHUDDER

I said well I don't know about MONSTERS but maybe there could be unicorns or pixies or tree elves.

Greg said there's no such THING as tree elves but I'm pretty sure there ARE because one time me and my dad spotted one during a backyard campout.

When I asked Greg how he's so SURE
there's no such thing as tree elves he
said the same thing he ALWAYS says to
win an argument.

Greg said if I'm gonna put PIXIES in the
story then there should be TROLLS too
because trolls EAT pixies.

I told Greg that was disgusting but he
said it's just the Circle of Life and I
needed to grow up.

CHAPTER 4

The villagers kept adding stuff to the list
of things they needed help with but after
a week Roland told them that him and
Garg really needed to get going so they
could save his mom.

And the villagers said OK but after you
guys rescue Roland's mom maybe you can
all come BACK and then she can help out
TOO. So Roland promised he'd talk to his
mom about that after he saved her and he
said goodbye to his new friends.

Then Roland and Garg left the village
and took a shortcut through the Tangled
Forest.

Roland was nervous about leaving the main road behind and going into the wilderness. The trees in the Tangled Forest were scary and it was super spooky in the dark woods.

And Roland knew there was probably no such thing as tree elves but he kept checking for them anyway.

The further Roland and Garg went into the woods the scarier it got. But before long they came to a clearing and were in a beautiful enchanted pixie village.

The pixies welcomed Garg and Roland to their village and brought them bowls of wild mushroom soup. And even though Roland didn't really like mushrooms he ate most of his soup anyway because he didn't want to be rude.

Roland told the pixies their village was beautiful and they said yeah that's because we live in harmony with nature and we don't have garbage piled up everywhere like those filthy trolls.

And when Roland said it wasn't NICE to call someone filthy the pixies said yeah well wait till you MEET them.

The pixies asked Roland and Garg what they were doing in the forest and Roland said they were taking a shortcut to rescue his mom from the White Warlock.

So the pixies told Roland they were sorry
to hear about his mom but if him and Garg
were going to defeat the White Warlock
they'd need WEAPONS.

So Roland told them he didn't really
BELIEVE in fighting because his parents
always taught him if he was nice to
someone they'd be nice BACK. And the
pixies thought that was pretty hilarious.

After they finished laughing the pixies
said you guys should have weapons "just
in case".

Then the pixies brought Garg a giant spiked club to use for smashing things.

They told Roland they knew where there was a sword that would be PERFECT for him but the problem was that it was stuck in a ROCK.

So they took Roland and Garg deep into the forest to show them.

The pixies told Roland that Bampy the Brave once came through these woods and drove his sword into the rock. And legend said that only someone with a pure heart could get the sword UNSTUCK.

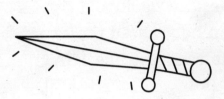

Garg tried to pull the sword out of the rock but even with all those muscles the sword didn't BUDGE.

The pixies told Roland maybe HE should give it a try. But Roland knew it wouldn't work because he wasn't even HALF as strong as Garg.

Roland decided he should try ANYWAY. And when he grabbed the sword it came out of the rock just like THAT.

Then Roland realized it meant he was pure of heart. And that made him feel proud because it proved his parents raised him RIGHT.

When Greg read the latest chapter he had some thoughts on the whole sword thing.

Greg said it was TOTALLY unrealistic that Roland could pull the sword out of the rock when Garg COULDN'T. He said Garg probably LOOSENED it and that's why Roland got it out so easily.

Then I told Greg the sword was MAGICAL and it had a whole STORY behind it. I said the sword was forged in the fires of Mount Friendly by a wizard named Walter the Wonderful.

Greg asked me what the NAME of the sword was because he said a magical sword needs a name.

So I said "Jeremy" because it was the first thing that came to mind. But I wish I'd taken my time and come up with something a little BETTER because maybe then Greg wouldn't have laughed so hard.

Then Greg asked me what the sword's magical powers were and I said it had the power to turn bad guys NICE. And he thought that was pretty hilarious too.

Greg said maybe the sword should do something COOL like shoot lightning from its tip.

But I liked my idea better because it was
more ORIGINAL.

Greg said if I care about being original
then I can't have Roland pulling a sword
from a stone because there's already a
MOVIE about that.

And I said it's not a stone it's a ROCK so
Greg said well good luck getting sued.

Then Greg said at least the characters finally had some WEAPONS because we could make them into TOYS.

I said I didn't think that was such a good idea because a kid could get hurt playing with them and parents wouldn't like that. But Greg said if they were Nerf toys then kids could totally clobber each other and their parents wouldn't even CARE.

CHAPTER 5

After Roland and Garg said goodbye to their pixie friends it was really dark out so it was hard to see where they were going. And the next thing they knew they were tumbling down a HILL.

When they finally got to the bottom they were surrounded by TROLLS. And Roland would never say it out loud but the trolls really were kind of filthy.

The trolls took Roland and Garg to their leader who sat on a giant throne made of GARBAGE. And Roland thought for sure the trolls were going to cook Roland and Garg in a STEW.

But the troll king was actually pretty
NICE. He said sorry this place is such a
dump but it's really not our FAULT.

The troll king told Roland and Garg that
every night the pixies toss their garbage
down the hill and it all ends up in Troll
Town.

He said the reason the trolls were so filthy
was because they spent all their time
trying to clean up the pixies' GARBAGE.
Plus the trolls didn't really believe in
taking baths so there was that too.

Then the troll king said the pixies brag that they live in harmony with nature but they're really just a bunch of PHONIES who dump their trash on someone ELSE.

Well if there's one thing Roland didn't like it was LITTERING. So he marched back up the hill with some trolls to talk to the pixies.

The pixies weren't happy to see trolls in their enchanted village and they weren't shy about SHOWING it either.

Roland told the pixies they had to stop dumping their trash in Troll Town because littering is WRONG.

But the pixies said the REASON they dump their trash in Troll Town is to get back at the trolls who are always sneaking up the hill and EATING them.

And when Roland asked the troll king if this was TRUE he said yes but trolls can't HELP eating pixies because they're so DELICIOUS.

So Roland came up with an idea to make PEACE between the trolls and the pixies. He said if the trolls promised not to eat any more pixies then the pixies had to stop throwing their trash into Troll Town.

And the troll king and the leader of the pixies thought that sounded fair so they did a pinky swear to make it official.

Then Roland taught everyone how to deal with trash PROPERLY and there was finally peace in the Tangled Forest.

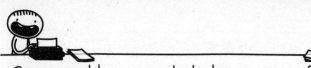

Greg said he was glad there were finally some actual MONSTERS in the book but he wasn't crazy about the recycling stuff. He said kids don't want books with MESSAGES in them these days so I was probably gonna have to cut that part.

But I said I wanted to have a BUNCH of messages in the story like "say no to bullying" and "save the planet" and "believe in the magic of Christmas". But Greg said kids don't want a bunch of lessons they want ACTION.

Greg said I should rewrite that last chapter so it was a BATTLE between the trolls and the pixies and then we could make it into an awesome VIDEO GAME.

But my parents don't let me play violent video games so I said maybe we could do something they'd APPROVE of.

Greg said OK forget about the trolls and the pixies and let's talk about what monsters Garg and Roland are gonna face NEXT. And he pulled a book off his shelf about ancient mythology and we looked through it together.

I told Greg we couldn't use any of the monsters in the book because that would be copying somebody else's ideas.

But Greg said the people who came up
with those monsters died a long time
ago so ANYONE can use them now. Then
he told me there are a lot of OTHER
characters that have been around a while
so we could use them TOO.

So my next chapter is gonna have a
BUNCH of monsters and other new
characters in it. But I hope Greg's not
pranking me on this one because I really
don't wanna get SUED.

CHAPTER 6

After Roland and Garg left the Tangled Forest they headed east across the Salt Flats. And nothing exciting happened there so let's just fast-forward to when they got to the mountains of the Razor Range.

The mountains were much too steep to climb so Roland and Garg travelled north towards the Boulder Pass. But they didn't get far because there was a terrible thunderstorm and they had to find SHELTER. Luckily there was a cave nearby and they went inside to wait out the storm.

It was dark in the cave so Roland lit a torch. And that's when he came face to face with a MINOTAUR.

But if you're like "Uh-oh Roland is about to get eaten by a Minotaur" well guess what you're WRONG. It was just a STATUE of a Minotaur.

When Roland's eyes adjusted to the torchlight he could see that there were a bunch of OTHER statues in the cave.

Roland didn't recognize all the statues but he did recognize a FEW of them like Huckleberry Finn and the Cowardly Lion and even Thor the God of Thunder.

Roland thought maybe this was a MUSEUM and they shouldn't touch anything. But Garg was pretty eager to try out his new club and the statues gave him a good excuse.

Roland didn't really approve because it felt like littering and you already know how he feels about that from the LAST chapter.

Garg was about to smash a statue of a guy holding a magnifying glass and a pipe but all of a sudden the statue CAME TO LIFE. And that's when Roland realized it wasn't a statue at all.

It was the legendary detective SHERLOCK
HOLMES!

Roland asked Sherlock Holmes what he
was doing in this cave. And Sherlock
Holmes said he was trying to solve the
mystery of why so many people were
going missing in the Razor Range and the
clues brought him HERE.

Roland asked Sherlock Holmes if he ever
solved the mystery and he said yeah
everyone who went missing got turned
into statues by MEDUSA.

Well that totally spooked Roland and he
told Garg they should get OUT of there.
But Sherlock Holmes said to stay perfectly
still because Medusa was getting out of
the shower right at that MOMENT.

So Roland and Garg and Sherlock Holmes
acted like statues and closed their eyes
real tight when Medusa slithered by.

But Garg must've got curious because he
PEEKED right before Medusa went into
her bedroom and he got turned into a
statue.

CRICCKK

Sherlock Holmes told Roland they should
HIDE before she came back out so they
snuck into Medusa's bathroom and closed
the door behind them.

But Roland wished they had snuck out of
the front of the cave INSTEAD because
now they were TRAPPED.

Sherlock Holmes started using his detective skills to get them out of this jam and sure enough he found a CLUE. He said Medusa didn't have a MIRROR in her bathroom so that meant she couldn't look at her own reflection or SHE'D get turned into a statue.

Sherlock Holmes said all they needed to do was find a mirror. Roland remembered that Garg always carried one WITH him because he liked to look at his muscles whenever he got a chance.

So Roland snuck back out and searched through Garg's bag for the mirror.

But Roland was making a lot of noise
digging through the bag and Medusa
came out of her bedroom to see what was
going on.

When Roland found what he was looking
for he aimed the mirror at Medusa. But
she must've seen this trick BEFORE
because she reflected her image BACK
with a metal shield.

Right at that moment Sherlock Holmes
stepped out of the bathroom to see what
was taking Roland so long. And that's how
the world's greatest detective got turned
to STONE.

HISS HISS HISS

CRICCKK

Roland knew that if he opened his eyes he was going to be NEXT. So when Medusa tried to trick him, Roland kept his eyes shut TIGHT.

Then Medusa pretended like she left the room but Roland knew she was still there because he could hear her SNAKES.

Roland couldn't keep his eyes shut FOREVER so he tried to think of what his friend Sherlock Holmes would do to get out of this mess. Roland thought about Medusa's angry snakes and then he had an IDEA.

Roland told Medusa the reason her snakes were so MAD was because she was using a harsh shampoo that bothered their EYES. And then Roland told Medusa he had a travel bottle of GENTLE shampoo in his bag and maybe if she used it to wash her hair the snakes would calm down.

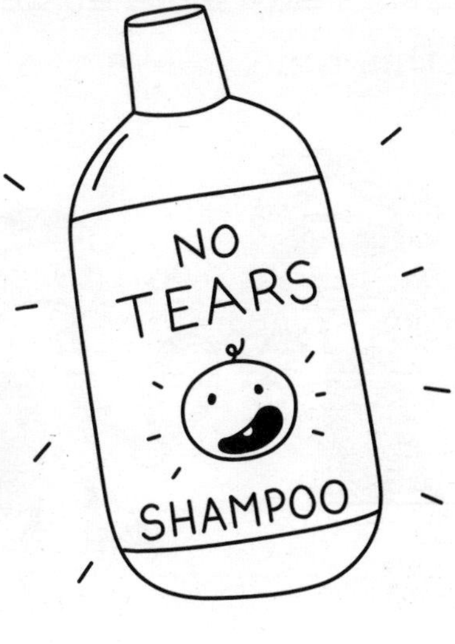
NO
TEARS
SHAMPOO

Well Medusa thought this was some kind of TRICK but Roland told her his parents raised him right and he never fibs.

So Medusa got the shampoo from Roland's bag and took her second shower of the day. And when Medusa came out she sounded happy and told Roland he could open his eyes because she put sunglasses on.

Roland wasn't sure how Medusa's parents raised HER and he thought this could be another trick. But Roland didn't hear the snakes hissing any more so he decided to trust her this time.

Medusa asked Roland if she looked pretty NOW. But Roland remembered his mom telling him that if you don't have anything NICE to say you shouldn't say anything at all.

So that's what he did.

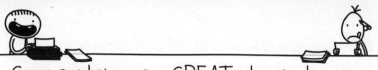

Greg said it was a GREAT idea to have all those characters from classic books in the last chapter because librarians go NUTS for that stuff. Then he said if we replace Roland with a character people have actually HEARD of we'd sell a lot more books.

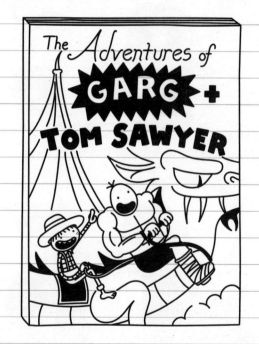

The Adventures of GARG + TOM SAWYER

Greg liked having Medusa as a character because everyone would know who SHE was.

And he said we could sell lots of toys like one that lets girls style her HAIR.

And I said maybe boys could play with it too if they liked that kind of stuff.

The only thing that made Greg nervous was how Sherlock Holmes had a PIPE because he said grown-ups get touchy about that and they might not sell the book at school fairs.

But I told Greg the pipe was just part of Sherlock Holmes's detective costume and didn't have anything IN it. And Greg said we should be OK then.

CHAPTER 7

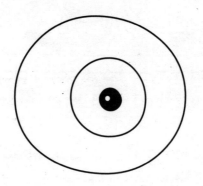

Medusa thanked Roland for the shampoo and told him he was free to go. But Roland knew he couldn't leave without his best friend Garg and his NEW friend Sherlock Holmes.

Roland asked Medusa if she could turn them back to normal but she said only a WIZARD could do that. And the only one she knew was the One-Eyed Wizard who lived in the Burnt Swamp.

So Roland left Medusa's cave to search for the One-Eyed Wizard. And even though Roland was scared to be on his own for the first time he tried to be brave for his mom.

The Burnt Swamp was even more awful than Roland imagined and he got totally LOST. But then Roland saw a light coming from a hut deep in the swamp and he went towards it.

Sure enough the hut belonged to the One-Eyed Wizard who told Roland to come inside and take a seat.

Even though Roland's parents told him to never talk to strangers he figured they'd let him make an exception this one time.

The One-Eyed Wizard said he had been
watching Roland for a long time in
his crystal ball and he knew all about
Roland's mom and the White Warlock
and Medusa and Garg and even Sherlock
Holmes.

And even though Roland was a little
creeped out that this guy had been
watching him all this time, Roland was
kind of glad he didn't have to tell him the
whole story from the beginning.

The wizard said the White Warlock wanted
to make it winter FOREVER and the
reason he kidnapped Roland's mom was
so he could make her his QUEEN.

Roland said the White Warlock COULDN'T make his mom his queen because she's already married to his DAD. But the One-Eyed Wizard said the White Warlock could just snap his fingers and make his mom forget all about her old life.

Then he told Roland the WORST part. He said Roland would be the White Warlock's STEPSON and he'd make Roland play catch with him and call him "Dad".

But the One-Eyed Wizard said there was
still time to save his mom because the
White Warlock couldn't make her his
queen until there was a crescent moon.
And that was still ten days away.

The One-Eyed Wizard said the Ice Fortress
was protected by a wall that was twenty
feet thick and thirty feet high. And nobody
had ever got THROUGH it before.

But Roland knew a guy who was good at
smashing things. And right now he was a
statue in Medusa's cave.

Greg said the new chapter was pretty boring because it was basically just two dudes talking in a swamp.

But when I said maybe I could add some more ACTION he said I should just keep it the way it is because this will be the scene in the movie when everyone gets up to use the bathroom and goes to refill their sodas and popcorn.

Then he said the BIGGER problem was
that there were way too many GUYS
in the story. I said MEDUSA is a girl
but Greg said she doesn't really count
because she's a MONSTER.

He said I need to put a few REGULAR
females in the story to give girls a
reason to come see the MOVIE. Because
if we DON'T, we'll only make HALF the
money.

Greg's other big comment was that the
"endless winter" thing has been done a
million times in other stories and I need
to change it to something ELSE.

I said maybe the White Warlock can make an endless SPRING instead. But Greg said that was the worst idea he ever heard because everybody LIKES spring.

So I guess I'll just keep it winter unless I can think of another season everyone HATES.

CHAPTER 8

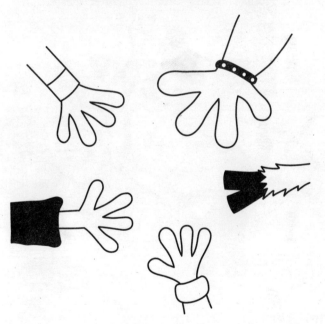

When Roland and the One-Eyed Wizard got to Medusa's cave she wasn't there. But she left a note that said she went off to New York City to become a model.

Roland showed the One-Eyed Wizard the statue of Garg, and the wizard used his wand to turn him back into a regular barbarian.

The One-Eyed Wizard turned Sherlock Holmes back to normal too. And then the wizard kind of got on a roll and unfroze everybody ELSE.

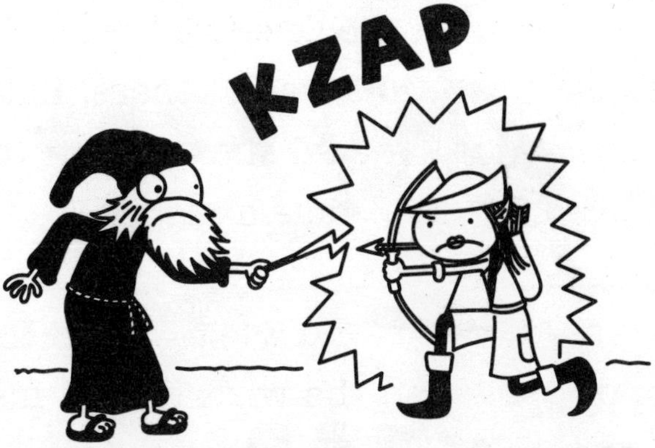
KZAP

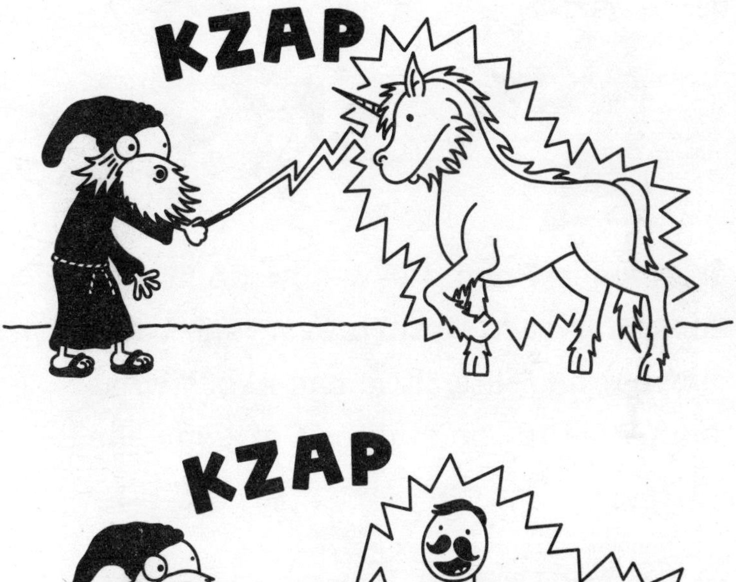
KZAP

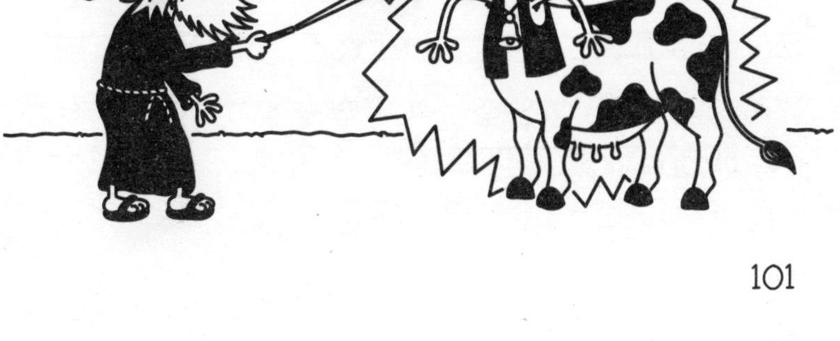
KZAP

And when Roland saw how EASY it was for the wizard to turn everyone back to normal he felt a little bad about what happened to the statues Garg smashed.

Most of the creatures hurried out of the cave in case the modelling thing didn't work out for Medusa and she came BACK.

But a few of them stuck around because they wanted to thank Roland for saving them and hear how he GOT there.

So Roland told them about his mom and the White Warlock and the stuff about the endless winter.

Then the elf girl said she'd come WITH Roland to help him rescue his mom. Then everyone ELSE said they'd go TOO.

And that made Roland happy because he knew his mom would be proud of him for making so many new friends.

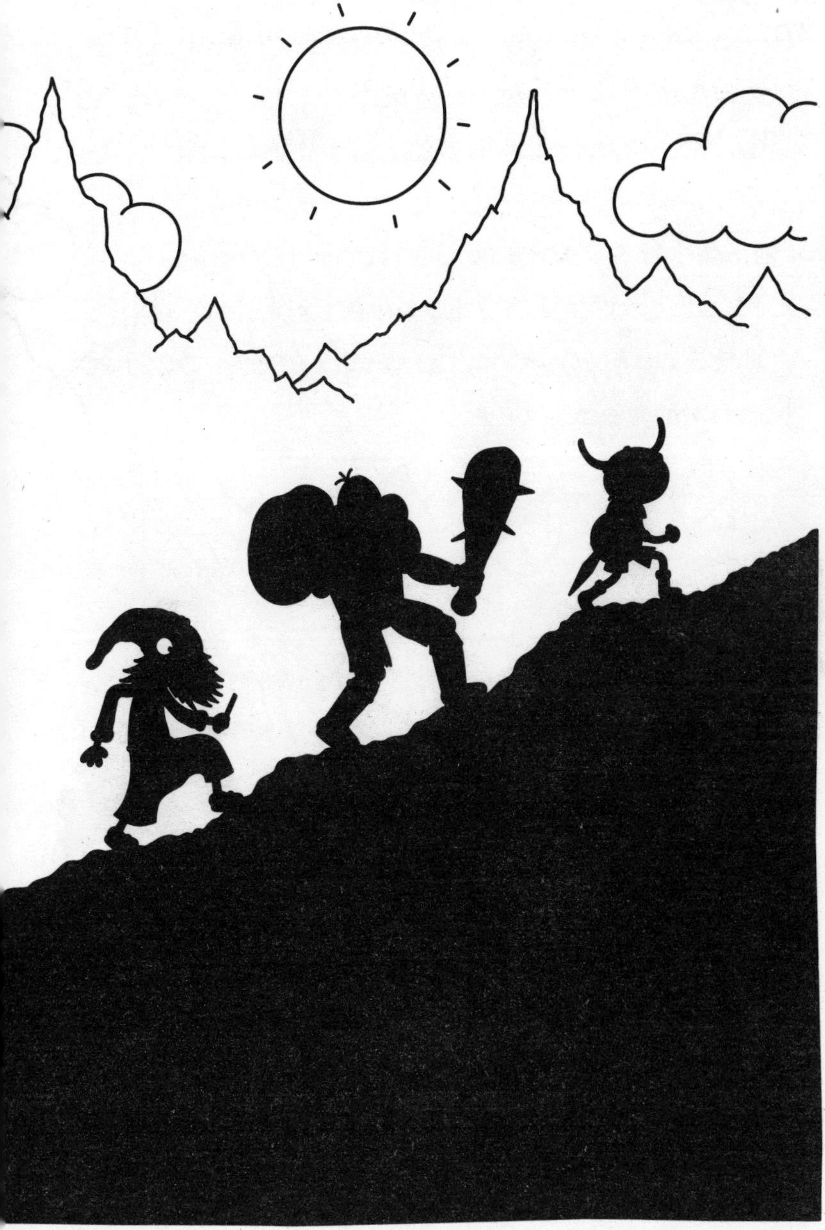

Greg said this was another boring chapter because it was mostly talking. But what he DID like were all the new CHARACTERS.

He said it's really important to have lots of characters so when the movie comes out you can do a different poster featuring each one.

Plus he said we could make little plastic figurines of all the characters and put them in those kids' meals you get at fast-food restaurants.

Well I didn't really like THAT idea because I don't wanna encourage kids to eat fast food. But Greg said kids could always swap french fries for apple slices and that made me feel a little better.

I also said I don't wanna add a lot of plastic junk to the world because that stuff hurts the PLANET.

So Greg said we could make the toys out of BIODEGRADABLE plastic so they'd turn to mush after a little while. And that made me feel better too I guess.

Greg really liked the girl elf whose name is Shae'Vana. He said girls would think she was cool and they'd all wanna dress up as her for Halloween.

Greg said Shae'Vana should have a special TALENT and that maybe she could be a master THIEF. I said stealing is WRONG but Greg said it's OK if it's her job. And I guess that kind of makes sense.

But Greg wasn't crazy about some of the OTHER characters in this chapter. He said I should ditch the alien because this book is supposed to be FANTASY and not sci-fi.

And Greg didn't like the half-man, half-cow whose name is Stephen.

Greg said if I was trying to draw a CENTAUR then it's supposed to be half-man, half-HORSE. I said I'm pretty sure centaurs can be cows too and he said yeah but all cows are GIRLS so if I wanted to keep it as a half-cow then Stephen would have to lose the moustache.

I said this was getting too complicated so maybe I'll just ditch Stephen too. But Greg said we should KEEP him because those udders are gonna come in handy when we do our fast-food deal.

CHAPTER 9

Roland and his team went through the Boulder Pass to cut across the Razor Range. That's where they were attacked by ogres who threw giant rocks down on them. And Roland was really glad he remembered to wear his helmet.

Everyone thought they were going to get squished by the boulders but then the One-Eyed Wizard created a giant magical hand to PROTECT them.

After they got clear of the Boulder Pass
the team was so happy to be alive that
they took a minute to CELEBRATE with
cold glasses of milk. And everyone agreed
it tasted WAY better than a sugary drink
like soda.

But they celebrated too SOON because five
seconds later they all got scooped up off
the ground by giant EAGLES.

At first Roland thought it was kind of
FUN to be that high in the air. But then
he realized the eagles wanted to feed
them to their BABIES.

Luckily Shae'Vana was really good with her BOW and she SAVED everyone. And the magical hand caught each of them and set them all down on the ground safely.

So now everyone was calling the magical hand "Lefty" and giving high fives and fist bumps to thank him.

And that made Lefty feel good.

Everyone thought it was too dangerous to stay out in the open so they decided to cut through the Mines of Murlak. But after everybody was inside, Garg hit his head on a stalactite which made the tunnel COLLAPSE.

So now they were TRAPPED and the only way OUT was to go all the way through the mines to the other SIDE.

After walking in the dark tunnels for a long time Roland and the team reached a giant underground lake. At first they thought they were totally STUCK because half of them couldn't SWIM.

But the lake was only a few feet deep so they waded through it. And when they got to the other side they were totally covered in GIANT LEECHES.

SCREAM!

Roland was pretty freaked out because once when he went to summer camp he got a leech on an embarrassing place and his mom had to come and bring him home two days early.

Luckily it wasn't that big a problem this time because the One-Eyed Wizard shrivelled up all the leeches by zapping them with his wand.

But all that zapping made a lot of noise and now the team had a NEW problem because they were totally surrounded by creatures with GIANT EYES.

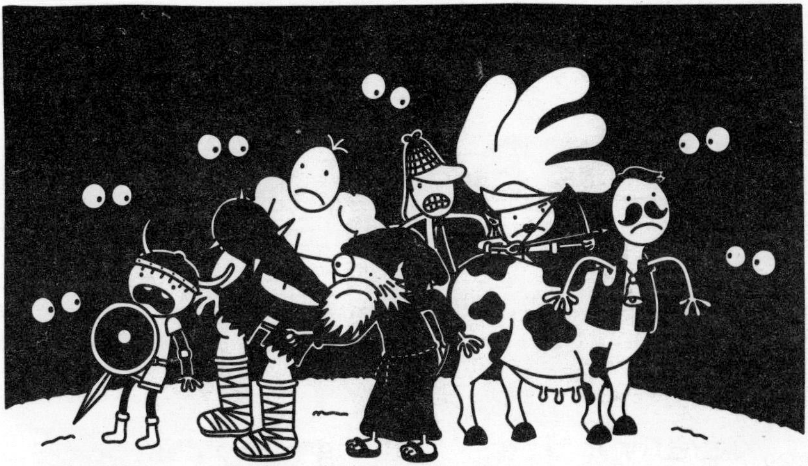

Everyone relaxed when the creatures came into the light and it turned out they were just DWARVES.

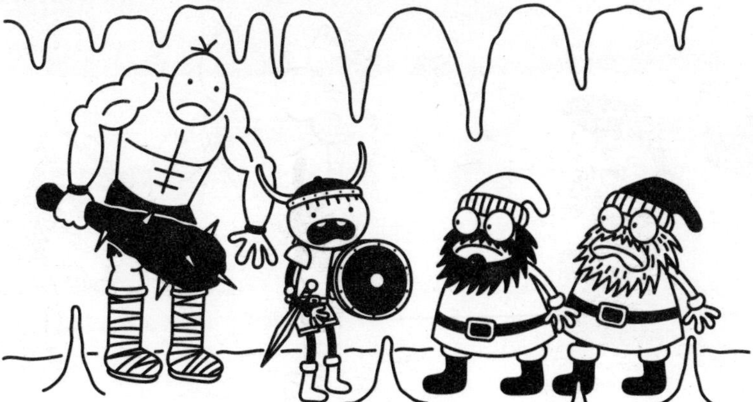

But the dwarves were MAD. They thought Roland's team was there to steal their JEWELS. So Roland and his friends hopped in mine carts to get away.

Then all of a sudden the tracks ENDED and Roland and his friends went flying through the darkness. Then they busted out of a WALL and landed on the ground outside.

The dwarves' eyes weren't used to the sunlight so they stayed back in the dark mines and yelled rude names and swears at Roland and his friends.

But Roland told his team to IGNORE the dwarves because they were just being BULLIES and bullies only want to get a REACTION.

And everyone agreed that was good advice.

Greg wasn't crazy about the anti-bullying message but he LOVED the mine cart scene. He said we could make it into an awesome theme-park ride and sell souvenir photos for thirty dollars a pop.

Greg said the only problem with the story NOW was that it wasn't FUNNY enough. He said every good story needs lots of laughs and so far this one has zero.

I said maybe I could add some knock-knock jokes in the next chapter but Greg said knock-knock jokes are the lowest form of comedy.

I said people ALWAYS laugh at my knock-
knock jokes and he said they're just
being POLITE.

So I said well then what DO people think
is funny? And Greg said body humour
like farts and burps and stuff. But that
stuff isn't funny to ME.

One of the rules in my house is that you
can't say "fart", you need to say "pass gas".
And another rule is that you're not allowed
to pass gas in the kitchen during meals.

Greg said if you're gonna write a book you HAVE to put in gross stuff or kids won't BUY it. And he said if we were REALLY smart we'd put something gross on the COVER.

Then Greg said he had an even BETTER IDEA. He said that nowadays a lot of books come with extra stuff like sticker sheets and mini posters.

So he said we could make a sticker sheet with a bunch of gross things on it so kids could add their OWN body humour wherever they WANTED.

Greg said we should throw in a lot of SLAPSTICK humour because kids love that kind of stuff too.

Then he told me this idea where the team pulls a prank on the One-Eyed Wizard by throwing his eye up on a wall. But that kind of sounded like BULLYING to ME.

Greg told me the OTHER thing the story is missing is ROMANCE. He said EVERY good book has some kind of love story in it so we'd better add one to OURS.

He said a good couple would be Garg and Shae'Vana because the elf would like Garg's MUSCLES.

And I said maybe Shae'Vana would like ROLAND because he's sensitive and has a shy smile.

But Greg said Roland's too busy practising his flute to be interested in girls so we should just go with Garg.

I said maybe we don't HAVE to put a romance in the story because it's OK for boys and girls to be FRIENDS. But then Greg said a BETTER idea would be to make Roland and Garg FIGHT over Shae'Vana.

Well I don't think it's good for two friends to fight over a girl so if there's gonna be a romance it'll have to be with someone NEW.

CHAPTER 10

After a whole day of adventures everyone was pretty tired. Nobody wanted to camp outside that night because they were worried some monster would come along and gobble them up while they were sleeping.

The One-Eyed Wizard said he heard about an old castle nearby that nobody lived in and maybe they could sleep THERE.

Everybody thought that sounded like a good idea except Roland who thought it actually sounded a little SCARY.

But it turned out the castle wasn't
abandoned after ALL. There was a light on
in the highest tower and everyone agreed
that someone should INVESTIGATE.

Shae'Vana volunteered and Roland
decided he would go WITH her. And when
they got to the base of the highest tower
Shae'Vana tied a rope to an arrow and
shot it up at the windowsill.

Shae'Vana climbed up the rope and Roland climbed AFTER her. And for the first time Roland noticed that she smelled like rose petals after a spring rain shower.

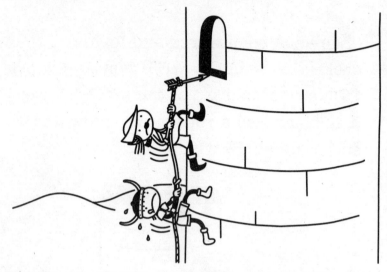

He thought maybe Shae'Vana used the same perfume as his MOM and was about to ask her. But by then they were already at the window.

Roland and Shae'Vana had to squeeze close together so they could both look through the opening. And that made Roland feel all warm inside.

But Shae'Vana didn't seem to notice because she was too focused on what was in the ROOM.

There was a teenager sitting on a bed and at first Roland thought it was just a person with pointy teeth. But then he realized this guy was a VAMPIRE.

Roland was about to tell Shae'Vana they both needed to get OUT of there but she had already climbed over the windowsill and into the room. And even though Roland thought this was a bad idea he FOLLOWED her.

The vampire barely even looked up at Shae'Vana and Roland. But when he finally noticed them he said they were his first visitors in three hundred YEARS.

The vampire said his name was Christoph and he got bitten by a vampire bat when he was a teenager. And after that everyone he loved got older and died but his curse was to stay the same age forever.

Christoph said after his parents passed away he locked himself in this tower so he would never bite a living soul.

He said he planned to stay in the tower
FOREVER. And Roland thought that
sounded like a GREAT plan.

When Christoph finally finished his story,
Shae'Vana asked him if he wanted to
come WITH them on their quest. And
before Roland could say anything the
vampire was already packing his things
for the trip.

Roland really wished Shae'Vana had
asked if it was OK to bring this guy along
BEFORE inviting him because Roland was
kind of the team leader. But he was a nice
guy so he didn't say anything.

The three of them climbed down the rope and Shae'Vana introduced Christoph to the whole team. And then the vampire said there was one thing he should mention before they got going.

He said he could only travel at NIGHT because vampires get turned to ash if they're exposed to SUNLIGHT.

But Shae'Vana said that wouldn't be a problem because they could just sleep during the DAY and travel after dark.

And everyone was OK with that.*

* Except Roland

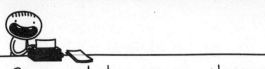

Greg said the vampire thing was GREAT
because teenagers love supernatural
romance stories and we needed to age
the story up ANYWAY.

He said girls would fall in love with the
vampire but guys would wanna BE him.
And he said he already had ideas for
personal fragrances and stuff like that.

I said maybe Roland could have his own
fragrance TOO. But Greg said the
vampire is a BAD boy and Roland is a
GOOD boy so it's just not the same.

Greg really liked the "curse" idea but the
truth is I got that one from HIM.

A few weeks ago Greg got mad at me
for not sharing my bubblegum and he said
he was gonna put a hex on me. And he
said that anything BAD that happened
from that point on was because of his
CURSE.

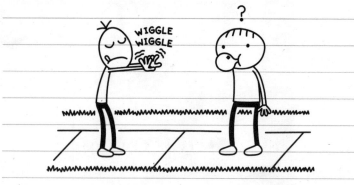

So I told Greg's mom what he did and she
made him REVERSE his curse.

But a few days later I stubbed my toe on a kerb so I'm pretty sure Greg only PRETENDED to reverse the hex.

Anyway Greg said that right now was the perfect time to shake the story up with a big PLOT TWIST. Well I thought the vampire WAS the plot twist so now I've gotta come up with something even BETTER.

CHAPTER 11

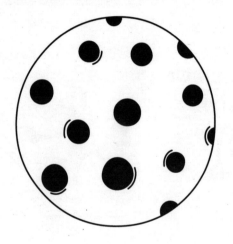

The team travelled at night and slept all day and everybody's sleep schedules were totally screwed up just so this vampire guy could go WITH them. And he didn't really ADD anything to the team unless you want to give him bonus points for not BITING anyone.

Roland told everyone they should all keep their hands free so they could get to their weapons if they got ambushed. But Shae'Vana and the vampire pretty much ignored him.

One night the moon peeked out from behind a cloud and the vampire started acting all WEIRD.

Then he transformed into a WEREWOLF right before their eyes.

Lefty had to hold the werewolf down so he didn't HURT anyone. And when the moon disappeared behind another cloud the werewolf turned back into a vampire.

Then Christoph told everyone the story of how he BECAME a werewolf.

So it turned out this guy had a DOUBLE curse. And that just seemed to make Shae'Vana like him even MORE.

Christoph said that as long as the moon was full he had to be inside or this would keep happening. So that meant now they couldn't travel at night OR during the day. And that was really annoying to Roland because he had already kept his mom waiting for long ENOUGH.

Roland took Shae'Vana aside and asked if maybe they should leave this guy behind because of the whole werewolf thing. But she said "this guy" had a NAME and his name was CHRISTOPH.

Then the One-Eyed Wizard said he knew a way to BREAK the vampire's double curse.

He said a ruby in the White Warlock's staff
had the power to REVERSE magic spells,
so if they could steal it they could turn
Christoph back into a regular PERSON.

Roland reminded everyone the whole
point of the mission was to rescue his
MOM and if the vampire got cured then
that was just a nice BONUS. But nobody
listened to him because all anybody
wanted to talk about was the RUBY.

The One-Eyed Wizard said that even if
they reached the Ice Fortress they still
didn't have a way IN because of the giant
WALL surrounding it.

So Shae'Vana asked Roland if she could see the MAP. Then she breathed on the section that showed the Ice Fortress and Roland thought her breath smelled like mint leaves dipped in honey.

A few seconds later some magic elf writing appeared on the map and Shae'Vana said it showed a SECRET ENTRANCE into the Ice Fortress.

Everyone was pretty excited but they all agreed it would be a good idea to get some rest before they made the final push to the Ice Fortress.

Roland was ESPECIALLY excited so he had trouble SLEEPING. At one point he reached for the map because he wanted to look at that cool elvish writing and maybe see if it still smelled like mint and honey.

But if you thought the werewolf thing was the big plot twist then guess what you were WRONG. Because when Roland reached for the map it was GONE.

Roland woke up Sherlock Holmes to see if he could figure out who TOOK the map. So Sherlock Holmes started looking for CLUES.

He said that first of all, there were elf footprints that led to Roland's sleeping bag. And second, Shae'Vana was MISSING. So Sherlock Holmes said Shae'Vana was the one who took the map and she probably did it to steal that RUBY.

Everyone was pretty amazed that Sherlock Holmes figured out the mystery so quickly. And he said he didn't want to brag but this was kind of an easy one.

Greg loved the plot twist but said he should get CREDIT for it because he was the one who said the elf should be a THIEF. But he didn't WANT credit because he didn't wanna have to deal with the BACKLASH.

Greg said that girls are gonna be really mad that the cool elf girl is BAD. He said when this book gets published I'm gonna have a bunch of people marching in my front yard and I'll never be able to go outside AGAIN.

And that made me really nervous because I just started tap-dancing lessons again and I need to leave the house on Tuesday and Thursday afternoons.

Greg said it's a risky move to create a character everyone likes and then switch things around so they're BAD.

He said a pregnant woman might read half the book and decide to name her baby Shae'Vana, and then find out her kid's named after a CRIMINAL.

I said maybe Shae'Vana can learn her lesson at the end of the story and tell kids that stealing is WRONG. But he said that's kind of corny and people will still be MAD.

I decided being an author is too much trouble and said I was just going to focus on tap dancing instead. But Greg said I can't quit NOW because the story isn't OVER.

Greg said I'm doing everything RIGHT but now I need to add a lot more DRAMA.

He said the characters should get into arguments and really go at it with each other because everyone loves watching people FIGHT.

I said the reason the team gets along so well is because they're all FRIENDS and they LIKE each other. But Greg said if everyone's always getting along then nobody's gonna CARE about the characters.

Plus he said this is supposed to be an ADVENTURE story that's full of danger but nobody's even got HURT. I reminded Greg that Roland got a blister in Chapter Three but Greg said that wasn't an injury it was just a first-aid thing.

So I said maybe the blister can get INFECTED but Greg said nobody wants to read a book about Roland's medical issues.

He said if I REALLY wanted to make the story exciting I'd KILL OFF one of my characters. But I didn't like THAT idea because it would make people SAD.

He said a good story's supposed to make you feel a whole BUNCH of different emotions and if readers feel sad I'm just doing my JOB. Then Greg said someone ALWAYS dies in a story like this and all I needed to do was pick a character I didn't really care about.

I said I liked ALL my characters and I didn't want ANY of them to die. But Greg told me if I want to be a REAL writer I'm gonna have to start making some tough choices.

CHAPTER 12

It turns out the map wasn't the ONLY thing the elf stole. The One-Eyed Wizard put his eyeball next to his pillow when he went to sleep and now it was MISSING.

The One-Eyed Wizard said his eye was MAGICAL and he could usually see out of it even if the eye was far away. But he said the elf must've put it in her POCKET or something because he couldn't see ANYTHING.

Roland asked the wizard how he was going to get around since he didn't have any eyes left and the wizard said he'd be fine because he could get by on his sense of smell.

There was one OTHER thing that was missing, and that was Roland's BAG.

155

And that was really bad news because he had a bunch of food and supplies in it. So the team went through Garg's bag to see if he had any food in there. But all he packed for the trip was a bunch of weights for working out.

Now everybody started PANICKING because they were in the middle of nowhere and didn't have anything to EAT. So everyone started arguing about whose FAULT it was that their stuff got stolen.

The vampire said it was ROLAND'S fault for leaving the map out in the open. And the wizard blamed Sherlock Holmes for not figuring out that the elf was a thief SOONER. But Sherlock Holmes said he's a DETECTIVE and he only solves crimes AFTER they happen.

Then the vampire started blubbering because he missed his GIRLFRIEND. And Roland actually felt kind of BAD for him.*

* But not that bad

All of a sudden a FIGHT broke out
between Stephen and Garg, so Roland had
to put them BOTH in time-out.

Roland was sad because all his friends
were fighting but he was ALSO sad
because he felt like he wasn't doing a
very good job of being a LEADER. So he
made a suggestion box and told everyone
they could put their notes in the slot.

And even though Roland told them to be
honest with their feedback some of the
comments kind of hurt his feelings.

SNIFFLE

suggestions

But Roland knew they couldn't just stay
HERE or he'd NEVER rescue his mom. So
he told everyone to gather up their stuff
because it was time to head out.

Well nobody was crazy about THAT idea
because without the MAP they didn't
know where they were GOING.

Then Sherlock Holmes found the elf's
FOOTPRINTS leading out of camp. He
said they could just follow her trail which
should take them all the way to the Ice
Fortress. And since nobody had a BETTER
plan that's what they did.

The elf's footprints led the team across
a grassy plain and to a cornfield where
there was a pathway cut into it. But the
path was twisty and there were lots of
places where it split in different directions.

Sherlock Holmes tried to follow the elf's
trail but it was HARD because the tracks
crossed over each other in some places.

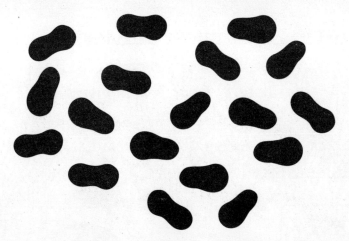

Sherlock Holmes stopped and told everyone they'd been TRICKED. He said this was a MAZE and the elf must've gone in here because she knew she'd be FOLLOWED.

Now they were LOST. Roland didn't know what to do so he closed his eyes and asked Bampy the Brave for HELP. And a few seconds later Roland heard a rustling noise in the corn.

And it was the GHOST OF BAMPY!

Bampy ran down a path and Roland and his team tried to keep up with him. They followed Bampy all the way out of the maze and then thanked him before he vanished back into the corn.

BAMPY!

Sherlock Holmes picked up the elf's trail
on the other side of the cornfield and the
footprints led down into a steep canyon
where there was a river of LAVA.

It was much too wide to jump across and
Roland knew he shouldn't ask Bampy for
help twice in one day.

But then Lefty picked everyone up one by
one and carried them to the other side of
the lava.

Just when the last team member got
across the lava river safely a GEYSER
shot up and blasted the magical hand.

And all anyone could do was watch Lefty
wave goodbye as he sank into the molten
lava and out of sight.

Greg said he was PROUD of me for writing that last scene because everyone's gonna be a MESS when they see it in cinemas.

He said the part about Bampy the Brave was kind of weird because people don't ask their dead grandpas for help. But I told Greg that sometimes when I lose things I ask MY Bampy for help finding them and he always DOES.

BAMPY!

Greg said he wanted to talk about which character should die NEXT. He said maybe it should be Stephen because he wasn't really adding anything to the story.

I said NOBODY else was gonna die because the story was ALREADY too sad. Greg told me I can't turn back NOW because the book is getting near the end and things need to get more and more SERIOUS from here.

But I think I need a BREAK from all this serious stuff so from now on I'm gonna tell the story the way I WANT to tell it.

CHAPTER 13

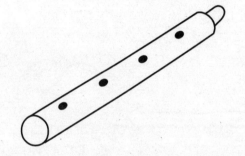

Everyone was really sad about Lefty so
they spent a lot of time crying on the lava
riverbank. But Roland was taking it the
hardest because Lefty was probably his
second-best friend after Garg.

The One-Eyed Wizard cast a spell for
ANOTHER magical hand but everyone
agreed it wasn't the same, especially
because this one was a RIGHTY.

Sherlock Holmes picked up the elf's trail again and the team followed it out of the canyon. But the tracks led to some dunes and then vanished in the sand.

So now they were all lost for REAL. And when the full moon came out the vampire turned into a werewolf and this time everyone just thought it was ANNOYING.

On the third night the moon started to CHANGE so at least they didn't have to deal with the whole vampire turning into a werewolf thing any more.

The team wandered across the sandy dunes for two nights hoping to pick up the elf's trail but they never DID. And they survived on cactus fruit and some gross insects Righty found under a rock.

Roland didn't know how much longer they could go on like this. One night they reached a winding river and set up camp. And while Roland was sitting by the fire the One-Eyed Wizard came over and sat next to him.

The wizard told Roland there would be
a crescent moon the next night and that
meant the White Warlock was going to
turn Roland's mom into his QUEEN.

That made Roland feel sad because
even though he had tried his hardest
he FAILED. And now it was going to
be winter FOREVER and his dad would
REALLY be disappointed in him.

So Roland walked down to the riverbank
and then pulled his flute out of his pocket
and played a sad tune.

All of a sudden Roland heard a splash
and noticed a MERMAID sitting on a rock
under the moonlight.

The mermaid said she liked Roland's song
and that he must practise a LOT. And
Roland asked her if she was the Little
Mermaid and she said yeah but not the
Disney one.

The Little Mermaid swam closer to
Roland and they had a really nice chat.

Roland told the Little Mermaid a knock-
knock joke and she LAUGHED. And Roland
could tell she wasn't faking.

Then they talked about all the famous
women they both admired like Amelia
Earhart and Jane Goodall and the one
who researched radioactivity.

But Roland said the woman he admired
the MOST was his mom.

And then Roland got SAD because he realized he might never SEE her again.

The Little Mermaid wanted to know what happened to his mom so he told her the whole story from the beginning. But he didn't mind because the Little Mermaid was a good listener.

When Roland was done the Little Mermaid told him that this river went straight to the Ice Fortress and if he followed it he'd get there in a few DAYS.

But Roland told her a few days was too LONG because it was going to be a crescent moon the next night.

So then the Little Mermaid pulled out her OWN flute and played a happy tune. And Roland thought that was kind of a weird thing to do right at that moment but he liked the song so he didn't say anything.

A few seconds later a NARWHAL came to the surface.

CHITTER CHITTER

The Little Mermaid told Roland the narwhal was her FRIEND and it could get him to the Ice Fortress before the crescent moon rose.

Then Roland told her about his team and said he couldn't go without THEM. So she played some MORE music and then MORE narwhals appeared. And before long Roland and his friends were on their way to the Ice Fortress.

I was really proud of this chapter because I liked how it teaches kids that if they listen to their parents and practise their instruments then good things will happen.

Plus I really liked the part with the narwhals and I told Greg we could put one on the COVER.

HOORAY FOR NARWHALS

But Greg said it was a TERRIBLE chapter and I was gonna have to make a TON of changes.

Greg told me the narwhal stuff felt way too YOUNG and if we put one on the cover then only little kids would buy the book. And he said he didn't wanna have to babysit a bunch of preschoolers at our book signings.

But I said I LIKED the narwhals. So Greg said maybe we could do an early-reader version of the book and a narwhal could be on the cover of THAT.

Greg said I should swap the narwhal for something COOLER like a seahorse because then OLDER kids would like it.

I said there aren't any seahorses in the story but Greg said that didn't MATTER because once someone buys the book you've got their money.

Then Greg told me it's not even that IMPORTANT what happens in the book since the people in charge of making the movie are just gonna change everything ANYWAY.

Greg said they were gonna have to make the story a lot more EDGY so teenagers would wanna see it. Then he said they'd probably replace Roland with someone who was twice his age and would say a lot of swears.

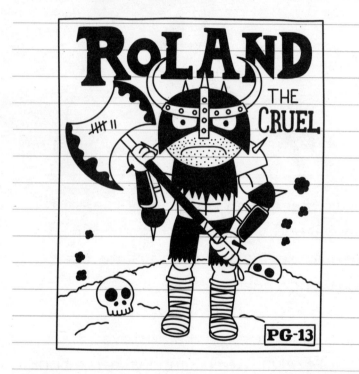

I said maybe we shouldn't even MAKE a movie if they're just gonna change everything.

And Greg said if there's not gonna be a movie then I could say goodbye to video games and personal fragrances and Halloween costumes and kids' meals at fast-food restaurants.

I told Greg I was OK with that because I was only trying to have fun and use my imagination and now everything was just getting too COMPLICATED.

So Greg said if we weren't gonna try to cash in on the book then he wasn't gonna help me FINISH it. And to be honest I was kind of OK with that too.

CHAPTER 14

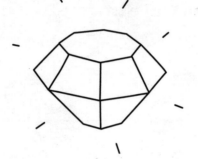

The narwhals took Roland and his friends all the way to the frozen shores of the Ice Fortress.

Roland's team said thanks to the Little Mermaid and the narwhals for getting them this far. And when Roland said goodbye to the Little Mermaid he gave her hand an extra squeeze to let her know he thought she was SPECIAL.

The Ice Fortress was surrounded by a thick wall just like the One-Eyed Wizard SAID it would be. Roland and the team started looking for the secret door but without that map they didn't even know where to START.

Then the One-Eyed Wizard stopped in his tracks. He said his magic eyeball must've fallen out of the elf's pocket because all of a sudden he could see EXACTLY where she was.

She was nearby looking for the secret DOOR.

The One-Eyed Wizard said they needed to move QUICKLY and find the door before the ELF could. So the wizard and Roland hurried off ahead of the rest of the group.

They ran along the ice wall and found the magic eyeball sitting on the frozen ground. But the elf was GONE.

The One-Eyed Wizard said she had probably already found the secret door and they were too LATE. And that made Roland feel really sad. But he was pretty tired from all that running so he leaned against the ice wall to rest.

Then the part of the wall where Roland put his hand started to GLOW and there was a loud rumbling noise.

It was the secret door! After it opened,
Roland and the wizard stepped inside the
tunnel.

They felt their way through the tunnel
until it started getting light up ahead.
And when they got to the end Roland
knew they were in the White Warlock's
THRONE ROOM.

The White Warlock was sitting on his
throne but Roland didn't see his MOM.

Roland had been waiting for this moment for a long time but now he was so scared he couldn't even MOVE.

The One-Eyed Wizard WASN'T scared though. He jumped out of the tunnel and stood in front of the White Warlock with his wand raised. But the White Warlock just LAUGHED.

HO HO HO!

Roland thought that laugh was really FAMILIAR. And that's when he realized the White Warlock was actually SANTA.

Roland was totally CONFUSED so he asked the One-Eyed Wizard what was going on. The One-Eyed Wizard explained EVERYTHING and it was kind of a long story.

The One-Eyed Wizard said Santa was his BROTHER. And when they were little boys their parents let them each pick a HOLIDAY to represent.

The One-Eyed Wizard said Santa was totally spoiled so he got to pick FIRST and of course he got the BEST holiday.

And when the One-Eyed Wizard picked HIS holiday he got one that nobody even CARES about.

So Santa went on to become world-famous because his holiday was AWESOME but the One-Eyed Wizard couldn't get people to care about his holiday even though he tried his hardest.

And then one day he got a little careless while waving a flag and he's been plotting revenge on his brother ever SINCE.

The One-Eyed Wizard said he knew he could never challenge Santa at the North Pole because his elves would PROTECT him. But he ALSO knew that Santa goes to the Ice Fortress to relax during the summer months so he hatched a plan to attack him THERE.

The One-Eyed Wizard said the only PROBLEM was that the Ice Fortress was protected by a giant WALL and the only way in was through a secret entrance.

Roland told the One-Eyed Wizard he kind of already KNEW this part but what the wizard said NEXT was a real surprise.

The One-Eyed Wizard said that only a person who was pure of heart could OPEN the secret door. And he'd spent YEARS searching for someone like that.

Then one day the One-Eyed Wizard was looking through his crystal ball and he saw a boy who was good and kind and loved his parents very much. And that boy was ROLAND.

The One-Eyed Wizard knew that if he tricked Roland into thinking his mom was kidnapped he'd go on a journey to SAVE her. And that would lead him right to the Ice Fortress and the secret door.

So the One-Eyed Wizard whipped up a snowstorm in Roland's village and when his mom went to the store to buy a snow shovel he hypnotized their next-door neighbour Mrs Nettles into telling Roland the made-up story about the White Warlock. And that's how this whole thing got STARTED.

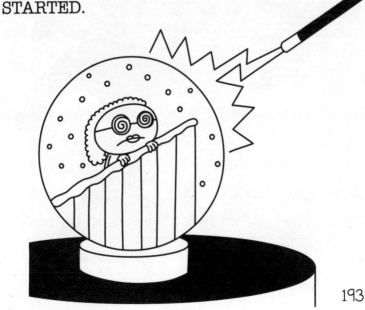

Then he said the story about marrying
the White Warlock and the endless winter
thing was all a big LIE.

At first Roland was HAPPY because this
meant his mom was safe and sound back
at home. But then he got SAD because he
knew his parents were probably worried
SICK about him.

And that made Roland MAD. So he pulled
out his sword and took a step towards
the One-Eyed Wizard. But now it was the
One-Eyed Wizard's turn to laugh. And
even his LAUGH wasn't as good as his
brother's.

The One-Eyed Wizard said the whole
reason he picked Roland to BEGIN with
was because he was too NICE to fight.
And Roland knew the wizard was RIGHT.

But now SANTA was mad and he WASN'T
afraid to fight.

Santa rose up off his throne and used his staff to shoot snowballs at the One-Eyed Wizard. But the One-Eyed Wizard was READY for that and he blocked them with a magic SHIELD.

Then the One-Eyed Wizard fired BACK by shooting FIREBALLS from his wand. But Santa BLOCKED the fireballs with icicles that fell from the ceiling.

Now the One-Eyed Wizard and Santa were face to face and they went at each other with everything they HAD. And Roland was worried because it seemed like Santa was LOSING.

But just when it seemed like the One-Eyed Wizard was going to WIN, an arrow came flying out of NOWHERE and knocked the wand from his hand.

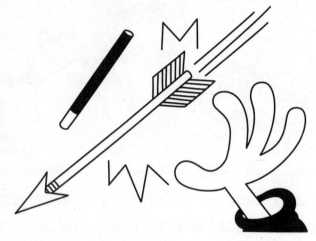

And Roland couldn't believe his eyes when he saw who SHOT it.

Shae'Vana shot three MORE arrows at the One-Eyed Wizard and pinned his robe to the ice wall so he couldn't MOVE.

Roland told Santa to look out because he thought Shae'Vana was going to shoot him NEXT. But Santa wasn't scared at ALL. In fact he seemed pretty happy to SEE her.

Now Roland was more confused than
EVER. But Santa and Shae'Vana explained
what was going on. And this was kind of
a long story TOO.

Santa told Roland that Shae'Vana was
one of his best toymakers and when she
was on holiday she got turned to stone
by Medusa. Then he thanked Roland for
SAVING her.

Shae'Vana said she figured out that the
One-Eyed Wizard was Santa's long-lost
BROTHER and knew she had to warn her
boss he was in DANGER. And she took
the MAP so the wizard couldn't find the
secret entrance HIMSELF.

Then she said she knew that stealing was
WRONG and wanted to apologize to any
kids who might hear about this somehow.

But everyone was too busy TALKING to
notice the One-Eyed Wizard had slipped
out of his robe and snuck up behind them.
And now he had Santa's STAFF.

HEE HAW
HEE HEE HAW
SNORT SNORT
SNORT!

The One-Eyed Wizard tried to blast Santa
with the staff but he MISSED and blew
holes through the throne room's icy walls
INSTEAD.

And that's how Roland's FRIENDS got in.

They started attacking the One-Eyed
Wizard and for a second it looked like the
good guys were going to WIN.

But just then Righty punched a hole
through the roof and the ceiling came
crashing down.

Then the evil magical hand snatched up everyone and held them in his sweaty fist. Roland thought for SURE they were all DOOMED. The hand squeezed tighter and tighter and Roland thought this was the END.

But just before he ran out of oxygen a MIRACLE happened.

It was Roland's MOM!

The One-Eyed Wizard was so surprised he lost his CONCENTRATION. And that made the magical hand lose his GRIP on Roland and his friends.

Now the One-Eyed Wizard was SUPER mad and he focused his attention on Roland's mom. He raised his wand and took a few steps towards her.

But Roland loved his mother very much so there was no way he was going to let anything HAPPEN to her.

Everyone was totally SHOCKED, especially Roland's MOM. But Roland knew his magical sword Jeremy had the power to turn bad guys NICE. And that's exactly what it DID.

The One-Eyed Wizard apologized to everybody for being such a jerk and they all FORGAVE him.

Roland asked his mom how she FOUND him and she said it was because of the NOTE he'd left for his dad back home. And then she thanked him for being such a thoughtful son.

Went to rescue
Mom from the
White Warlock.

−R

Santa said even though it wasn't Christmas yet he had a special PRESENT for each of them.

Roland's mom got a charm bracelet and Garg got a gift certificate to a tanning salon. Sherlock Holmes got a brand-new magnifying glass and the One-Eyed Wizard got a new flag with a rubber ball on the tip of the pole for safety. And Stephen got a Christmas jumper with a hole cut out for his udders.

Then Santa said he had an EXTRA-special present for Roland and gave him the biggest box of ALL.

But the box was EMPTY except for a rolled-up piece of paper at the bottom. So Roland opened it and read what was written on the scroll.

If a person has friends then they already have the best presents of all.

Roland thought the note was nice and all but to be honest he would've rather got a new TOY. But Roland was a polite boy and he didn't say anything because he wouldn't want to hurt Santa's feelings.

It turned out the note was just a PRANK and everyone else was IN on it.

And Roland didn't know how to feel about that because it felt a little like BULLYING.

Then Santa picked up Roland's sword and asked him to bend down on one knee. Santa said that Roland had proven himself on his quest so he earned a new NAME.

Then Santa tapped Roland on each
shoulder with the sword and knighted
him Roland the Kind.

Roland STILL probably would've liked a
toy instead, but his mom and his friends
seemed proud of him so that made
Roland feel better about the prank with
the note.

Santa asked the vampire if he wanted his double curse reversed but Christoph said he LIKED being a vampire-werewolf because girls think it's COOL.

Then Shae'Vana told Santa she was going to take some time off and travel with Christoph because her holiday kind of got cut short by the whole Medusa thing.

Everyone said goodbye to Christoph and Shae'Vana and wished them luck. And Roland was happy for them.*

Sherlock Holmes and Stephen told everyone they were teaming up to solve crimes together. So everyone wished them luck too.

* For real this time

And everybody who was LEFT got a ride
home with Santa on his magic sleigh.

When they got to Roland's house the
One-Eyed Wizard said goodbye and that
he was sorry again for all the trouble.

But Roland could tell the wizard was sad
to be leaving so he asked if he wanted
to live with him and his parents. And
Roland's mom said the One-Eyed Wizard
could sleep in Bampy's old room.

So everything worked out for everyone,
and Christmas that year was the best
one EVER.

THE END

I REALLY didn't wanna show the last chapter to Greg because I knew he'd have negative comments about all the Santa stuff. But Greg LOVED it.

He said the last chapter was GENIUS because now we could sell this book as a CHRISTMAS story. And he said those kinds of books do GREAT around the holidays.

I was a little worried because not everyone celebrates Christmas and I didn't want anyone to feel left out. So Greg said we could make lots of different versions so the story would work for EVERYONE.

The other thing Greg said we should do right away was trademark the word "kind". And then if anyone uses it in THEIR stories they'll have to pay us a ton of money.

But I think I'll let GREG deal with all that stuff. The truth is I don't really CARE if this book gets published because like I said I wrote it for myself ANYWAY.

Well not JUST myself. I hope my mom and dad like it too. In fact I think I'm gonna have my dad read it to me as my bedtime story tonight. Because I really like how he does different voices for all the characters when he reads me stories.

And if I accidentally fall asleep in my parents' bed halfway through the book, then I'm OK with that.

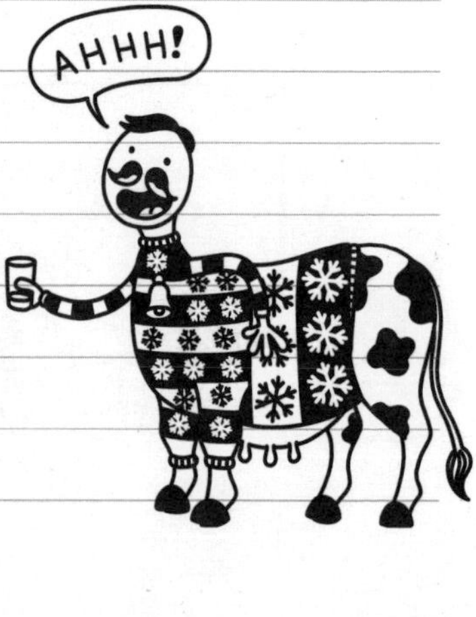
AHHH!

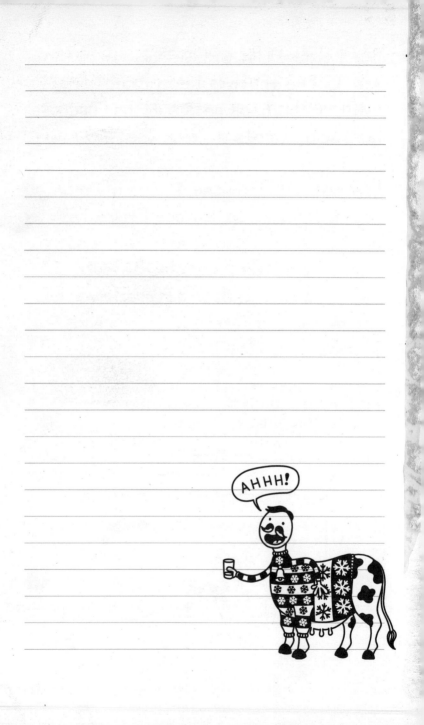